Prologue

Our world is only the beginning.
Beneath the surface and between the
moonbeams there is another place.
A place where the flowers sing and
birds and animals live happily with
the little people of Fairyland.

All the magic in our world comes
from this place, through doorways that
only the fairies can open. And, at the

centre of the magic is the Fairythorn Tree.

The Fairythorn, as the little people call it, is always the oldest tree in any garden, wood or park. It might be gnarled and spiky on the outside, but it is a comfortable home for the tiny fairies who live hidden inside its trunk and branches.

And if you look very closely, right down where the base of the trunk meets the mossy ground, you might just spot a doorway to the fairies' world.

Look very closely, now. It's even smaller than you think…

Chapter 1

It was the morning of Midsummer's Day and the sun was already a big, boiling ball of fire in the sky. The world below it looked like an endless, colourful patchwork quilt.

Every square was different. There were dark green squares of forest and yellow squares of tall, proud sunflowers and plump wheat. There were light-green patches of grassy meadows and brown squares of new-ploughed earth. The rivers were stitched in blue and the towns and cities glittered and gleamed like sequins as the sunlight bounced off steel and glass. But among all the millions of multi-coloured patches, there was one little square of land that stood out...

The Miller family's back garden was a jumble of colour. Flowers of every imaginable variety had exploded into life all over the place. They burst out of every available inch of soil, clambering up the sides of the shed and fighting for space along the borders of the tangled path.

At the bottom of this colourful garden, the Choir Fairies from the Fairythorn Tree were belting out the last verse of their Sunrise Song.

Among the mossy roots and secret places at the bottom of the tree, all sorts of fairies were also welcoming the new day. They were everywhere, sparkling as they fluttered about like tiny puffs of glitter, dancing in the air and playing homemade musical instruments.

Their dragling companions were in high spirits too, tumbling around and falling over each other like excited puppies as they mewled along to the music.

Fleur sat cross-legged on a daisy head, playing her guitar. As she concentrated on the chord she was playing, her red curls spilled across her face like a curtain of fire. She finished the tune and gave her guitar a stroke.

She'd carved it from a broken branch of maple, and the neck was a twig from the Fairythorn Tree itself.

Fleur loved to make musical instruments out of things she found in the garden. She'd made so many her bedroom was stuffed full.

As the Choir Fairies reached the end of their song, Fleur held her breath. The beautiful sound hung in the air for a moment, then it was gone.

Fleur let out her breath in a big sigh. She wished she could join the Choir Fairies, up there among the songbirds, singing their hearts out every day. But there was no way she could do that. Not after what had happened.

"Hey, Fleur! Come and join us!"

Two of Fleur's best friends, Honeysuckle and Rose, were dancing in a wide circle of fairies. Honeysuckle looked fabulous in a crown of oak leaves and freshly picked clover, while Rose had tied tiny silver bells around her ankles. Meanwhile, Posy, the last of the four friends, was lying back on small, flat rock, enjoying the music with her eyes closed.

Fleur hopped off her daisy and

headed in Posy's direction. Posy had been on Grot Goblin watch all night and was still clutching the magic golden horn which Mother Nature had hung around her neck.

Grot Goblins were nasty creatures who hated nature and did anything they could to destroy it. One sight or sniff of a Grot Goblin and Posy was to blow the horn and summon Mother Nature in a flash.

The fairies clapped and cheered as the music ended. Honeysuckle and Rose ran over to join Fleur and Posy. Their cheeks were bright pink from all the dancing and the bells at Rose's heels jingled brightly.

"Have you seen what that lot are up to now?" said Honeysuckle.

She nodded her head in the direction of their draglings, the dragon-like creatures that each fairy had as a companion. The fairies loved them, but the draglings often behaved like naughty kittens – kittens who could breath fire! At that moment the four draglings were splashing about in a muddy puddle and getting absolutely filthy.

"What lot?" said Posy, sitting

up on her rock
and rubbing
her eyes. She
glanced over

just as Dash skidded through the
puddle on his back, getting great,
soggy splodges of mud in his purple
fur.

"I only bathed him yesterday,"
Posy groaned. "Now he looks like he's
run a mud marathon!"

"Red gets muddy so often, I
sometimes wonder if he thinks he's a
hippo," said Fleur.

"I think the mud's good for their

fur or something," said Honeysuckle wisely.

"It's typical behaviour," said Posy, who was a Dragling Fairy, and spent her days training the creatures. "Whether we like it or not," she added, grinning.

Posy had only recently started her new job. Before that, she'd been waiting for her wings to unfurl so she could find out what kind of fairy she'd be. Not that long ago, to Posy's delight, her peacock-patterned, purple wings had revealed themselves. At the same time, her dragling, Dash, had

turned purple with green trimmings
– the colours he would stay now that
his fairy had her wings.

Rose and Honeysuckle sat side
by side on a broken twig and stretched
out their legs.

"I like your new guitar, Fleur,"
said Rose. She was a Wish Fairy, with
beautiful pink wings that looked just
like petals. Her dragling, Pax, was a
bright shade of pink.

"Thanks," said Fleur. She hadn't
got her wings yet, and she wished
they would hurry up. Fleur knew she
should be more like Honeysuckle,

who was waiting too, but was being much more patient about it.

Fleur played a few chords. "I asked a spider to spin me some strings," she said. "What do you think?"

"Sounds lovely," said Rose.

"Very spidery – in a good way," agreed Honeysuckle earnestly.

Fleur grinned and set the guitar aside. "Have you lot noticed the seeds we gave to the little Bigs have all sprung up overnight?"

Fleur and her friends had given the wildflower seeds to Alice, the little girl who lived at the end of the garden, and her best friend, Edie. The little Bigs, as the fairies called them, had scattered the seeds everywhere. As they had been touched by fairy magic, the seeds had sprouted within hours, turning the garden into a miniature meadow of colourful, sweet-smelling blooms.

"You know what," said Fleur, "I can't help thinking that a few Fairyland seeds got mixed in with the poppies and foxgloves."

"What do you mean?" asked Honeysuckle.

"Well," Fleur continued, "it's

just that I trod on a buttercup after breakfast and it got quite cross."

Honeysuckle nodded. "Talking buttercups? Oh dear! We'll have to keep an eye out — hopefully there won't be any troublemakers."

"The bees are enjoying the flowers though," said Posy. "Look how fat they've got!"

The friends stared up at the bees that were buzzing around their hive, built in a hollow in the trunk of the Fairythorn Tree.

"Let's hope they'll be generous with their honey for the Midsummer

Feast later," said Honeysuckle, licking her lips. "I bet it tastes delicious with all these flowers in the mix."

"I hope I get to help with the honey harvest," said Fleur, grinning.

"Me too!" Rose agreed, her eyes shining.

For fairies, harvesting honey was like going strawberry picking – they generally ate more than they actually collected. And the first full moon of Midsummer was always the best time to talk bees into giving away their precious honey as their hives were overflowing.

"Ooh, I hope we have honey marmalade at the feast," said Posy. "It's my favourite."

She was interrupted by a cloud of butterflies that swooped down over the garden. They fluttered over the long grass before coming together ever so briefly to form an image of Mother Nature's smiling face.

"Look out," said Posy, standing up straight. "Messengers have arrived."

Mother Nature often used butterflies to carry her messages from one fairy community to another when she was busy with other business. Fleur and her friends scrambled to their feet, eager to find out what Mother Nature wanted. Her message had to be important or she would have waited until she could give it to them in person.

One of the butterflies – a large

Tortoiseshell – landed gracefully on a primrose beside Fleur.

"I hope it's nothing bad," said Rose, frowning.

Chapter 2

With a series of carefully spaced beats of its red and black wings, the butterfly began to pass on its message. Other butterflies around the garden did the same.

The four friends concentrated, following the message from the Tortoiseshell closely. They were being told that Mother Nature wanted the Song Fairies to be at their very best for that evening's sunset – and if anyone else wanted to join the choir, they were more than welcome. The more beautiful the song, the more stunning the sunset, and Mother Nature wanted a spectacular performance to mark Midsummer's Night.

After the messengers had fluttered off to their next delivery, Rose turned to Fleur with a thoughtful look on her face.

"What's up, Rose?" asked Fleur.

"Are you sure you won't sing ever again, Fleur?" Rose asked, gently. "Your voice alone would make for the prettiest sunset ever."

Fleur sighed and slung the daisy-chain strap of her guitar over her shoulder. "Don't be silly," she mumbled.

"You've got the most beautiful singing voice of any fairy we know," said Posy. "It's like having wings and not letting yourself fly." She shuddered at the thought, and fairy dust puffed off her wings like glittery baby powder.

"It's fine," said Fleur, patting her guitar. "I can sing through my instruments."

"But doesn't it make you sad not

to use your voice?" Rose persisted. "You used to say that singing was like breathing to you."

Fleur tossed back her hair and stars flashed in it like tiny fireworks going off. "Consider me out of breath," she said firmly, narrowing her eyes and staring hard at her friends. "I'm not singing any more, and that's that!"

Rose opened her mouth to argue, then quickly shut it again. Fleur's temper could be as fiery as her wild red hair.

Fleur stuck her fingers in the corners of her mouth and whistled for her dragling. "Come here, Red," she called, "we're going."

She hopped off her daisy and headed towards the garden pond, Red scampering after her.

Fleur stomped through the shaggy grass with Red on her heels, muttering angrily to herself.

"It's not fair of them to keep going on at me like that," she grumbled. "They've made me feel selfish for not helping with the Midsummer Sunset Song. But it's not my fault. I just can't risk it."

She stopped suddenly and Red ran straight into the back of her legs. Fleur threw her hands up in frustration. "Who knows what would happen if I did?"

Everyone knew about the accident that had made Fleur stop singing. All the fairies had been there.

It was at the Christmas concert, six months ago. Everyone had been singing together and Fleur, showing off an incredible high note, had managed to dislodge a large icicle with the vibration of her voice. The icicle had been hanging from the branch of the Fairythorn Tree, and it fell like a hammer.

Miraculously, it had missed most of the fairies, but it did clip the wings of a Pollen Fairy, damaging them so badly that she couldn't fly any more. Fleur had felt so guilty, she had vowed never to sing again.

Red was mewling at her ankles for some attention. Fleur gave him a quick stroke, then trudged slowly forward to the pond. She sat down on a cracked flagstone at the water's edge and carefully laid her guitar to one side. Red curled up next to her.

"Oh, Red," Fleur sighed, stroking her dragling's soft green fur. "It's all so horrible. I want to sing, I really do… but I can't."

A fat tear rolled down her cheek and she wiped it away with the back of her hand.

"Not after what I did."

Chapter 3

"There you are!"

Fleur jumped. She had no idea how long she'd been at the pond, staring into the murky water. She looked up to see Rose, who fluttered down next to her on the flagstones.

Fleur took a deep breath. "Sorry for being such a drama queen."

Rose grinned. "We're used to it," she said with a wink. "No, *we're* sorry for going on at you like that. I just think you're a lot sadder these days, since you stopped singing."

Just then, the back door of the Bigs' house opened and the biggest Big charged outside.

The two fairies froze as Mr Miller strode down the garden path, scooping up his garden gnomes, Derek and Clive, along the way. Although the Bigs thought they were just concrete statues, Derek and Clive had been accidentally enchanted and could now talk.

The gnomes kept popping up all over the place, as the members of the

Miller family disagreed on where they should live. Mrs Miller thought they were ugly and preferred them out of sight behind the shed. But Mr Miller thought they looked their best by the pond, and that's where, Fleur guessed, he was off to now.

In a flash, Fleur and Rose dived into the undergrowth to hide. Red and Pax quickly slipped beneath a clump of flowers. But Mr Miller walked straight past the pond and kept on going – he was heading for the Fairythorn Tree.

Fleur stuck her head out from

behind a flower. It rested on her hair
like a bright yellow hat.

"What's that Big up to?" she said.

The friends slipped out from
their hiding place so they could get
a better view. Mr Miller had set Derek
and Clive down, side by side, right in

front of the Fairythorn Tree. He was standing back with his hands on his hips and a smile on his face.

"Oh no! He's not really going to leave them there is he?" said Rose. "They'll drive us mad!"

"I think he might," groaned Fleur. "Surely that counts as cruelty to fairies or something?"

"It probably would, except he doesn't know about us," sighed Rose.

They watched as Mr Miller took a couple of steps backwards and tilted his head to one side, frowning. Then he walked slowly round the tree, ducking his head under the low-hanging branches.

"What's he doing now?" said Rose.

"I'm not sure," said Fleur. She winced as she watched him pull a twig from the tree. "But I definitely don't like it."

Suddenly, Mr Miller grabbed an entire branch of the tree with both hands and yanked it down hard, snapping it right off. Rose screamed at the top of her lungs. Fleur's knees buckled. She stared at the ugly splintery scar that was left on the trunk of the Fairythorn. That was where Honeysuckle's bedroom was! There were twenty fairy bedrooms all lined up along the corridor inside that one branch.

Fleur and Rose froze in shock as the Big tossed the branch aside as if it were nothing, then stared back at the tree again, not realising the awful damage he'd done.

"That'll burn nicely on my bonfire," he muttered to himself. Then he marched over to his shed and disappeared inside.

Rose burst into tears.

"Do you think there was anyone in there?" she spluttered.

"They're probably still out and about after the Sunrise Song. Posy definitely will be," said Fleur. "But when did you last see Honeysuckle?"

Rose's face turned even paler than usual. "Oh no!" she cried. "Honeysuckle was going back to her room. She wanted to take off her oak-leaf crown before she started work for the day…"

Fleur whistled to a passing blackbird. They needed transport, quickly! The bird swooped down to land beside the fairies and nodded its head in greeting.

"Let's get over there," said Fleur, her stomach bubbling with fear. "Please take us to the Fairythorn Tree, blackbird. As fast as you can!"

Chapter 4

The blackbird reached the Fairythorn Tree with three flaps of its jet-black wings. It landed just a hop away from the broken branch, where a crowd of fairies and garden creatures were already gathering to stare at the destruction.

Draglings were circling overhead like seagulls over a shipwreck. Derek and Clive, the world's grumpiest gnomes, were standing right where

Alice's dad had left them, at the foot of the Fairythorn. They sounded like they were thoroughly enjoying the chaos that had broken out around them.

"Lot of fuss over an old twig," sneered Derek, ignoring the fairies' disapproving looks.

"Now, now," said Clive. "It's not just an old twig."

"No?" Derek said.

"No," said Clive, sniggering. "It's a *broken* old twig!"

The two dissolved into cackling laughter until a group of fairies flew into the air above them and dropped a dirty potato sack over their heads.

Fleur and Rose slid down from the blackbird and pushed their way through the crowd, in search of Honeysuckle and Posy. Fleur stopped to talk to a Cloud Fairy with velvety soft white wings.

"Was anyone hurt, Billow?" she asked anxiously.

"I don't think so," said the Cloud Fairy. "They're counting heads now."

Fleur nodded nervously and

looked around for Honeysuckle and Posy. There was no sign of them anywhere. "I can't see them!" she said to Rose, standing on tiptoes to scan the crowd again.

"They have to be here…" said Rose, who was always good at staying calm. "Somewhere."

Then her eyes widened and she let out a little squeak.

"What is it?" asked Fleur.

"On the ground," said Rose, pointing at the ground with tears in her eyes, "all bashed up. It's Honeysuckle's crown!"

Fleur followed Rose's finger to a crumple of oak leaves and clover poking out from underneath one end of the splintered branch. The two friends grabbed each other, and Fleur could feel Rose shaking.

"You don't think Honeysuckle's under there too, do you?" Fleur gulped.

"No, I'm not!" squeaked a furious voice from behind them. "But I wish that Big was! He's trashed my room!"

Fleur and Rose squealed and spun round to see Honeysuckle and Posy alive and well, but shaken and red-eyed from crying. The four friends bundled together in a big hug.

"Thank springtime that both of you are okay," said Fleur, as they moved away from the crowd to talk.

"Only just," said Posy, adjusting her wonky feathered headdress. "I popped back to Honeysuckle's room with her. We were only in there for a minute and were just coming out again when it happened. We only just missed getting squashed… There was no one else in the branch, thank goodness. It was horrible," she shuddered, "the whole tree sort of shivered, as if it was in pain."

"We thought it might be a Grot Goblin attack at first," said Honeysuckle. "So we just ran into the garden to come and help."

"I suppose we should be grateful there aren't Grot Goblins about," said Posy.

"Grown-up Bigs can be just as

bad though," muttered Fleur. "They're nothing but trouble."

"And now my bedroom is ruined," sighed Honeysuckle. She stared up at the branch and her bottom lip wobbled. "I'm homeless."

"Join the club," Derek mumbled through the potato sack.

"You and Pip can move in with me," said Fleur.

Honeysuckle pulled a face.

"What?" Fleur asked.

"I don't mean to be rude, but with all your musical instruments, there's barely enough room for *you* in there, let alone me and my dragling," Honeysuckle said. "Thanks, though."

"You can move in with me if you like," said Rose. "There's plenty of space for you and Pip. And Pax would love it."

"You'll get another room of your own soon, anyway," said Posy, putting her arm around Honeysuckle. "With a little work, whole new branches can be made ready to move into."

"And we can help you decorate," said Fleur. "I found an amazing shell the other day. It'll make a really pretty bed. We just need to find something soft to stuff it with, like dandelion clocks or bunny fur."

"And I can weave you a pair of spider-silk curtains," said Posy. "Any colour you want. Nettle juice will turn them the most amazing shade of green."

Honeysuckle smiled at her friends. "Thanks, you're all so kind. I know it's only stuff, but it was *my* stuff, and I'm still sad it's all gone." Her voice wobbled as she spoke and a tear rolled down her cheek. "My favourite shoes were in there. My ballet ones."

Honeysuckle was a wonderful

dancer, and she loved to twirl among the flowers on the tips of her toes. One day, Rose had found some doll's ballet slippers floating in a puddle and had cleaned and repaired them before giving them as a gift to her friend.

Fleur knew that, apart from Pip, they were Honeysuckle's favourite things in the world, ever.

"They might turn up," said Rose. "And if they don't, we'll find you another pair."

"Thanks, Rose, although I guess ballet shoes small enough for fairy feet don't come around very often," sighed Honeysuckle. "What do you think that horrible Big was doing, anyway?" she continued, staring over at the shed. Mr Miller still hadn't come out. "Apart from destroying my bedroom, I mean."

"That's exactly what I've been wondering," said Fleur.

"I heard him saying something about wanting a bigger shed," said Posy. "But I'm not sure what that has to do with the branch."

"Hee, hee."

"Tee, hee, hee!"

Through the potato sack came

the sound of giggling gnomes.

"You two spuds had better share the joke," snapped Fleur. "Or I'll make you into mash."

"You really are a proper flock of dimwits, aren't you?" said a voice through the sack.

"Think how tiny they are though, Clive," said a muffled Derek. "Think how small their brains must be."

"Oh, shut up and spit it out, you spiteful lumps of concrete," said Posy. "You know you can't wait to tell us. It's clearly something horrid."

There was a pause.

"It's obvious, really," Clive said eventually. "You couldn't fit a bigger shed where the old one's standing. You need a larger space. It's the perfect spot, right here where the tree is. So that means the tree has to go."

"Oh yes," said Derek. "Absolutely *has* to go. Chop chop."

Fleur's mouth dropped open as she turned to look at the horrified faces of her friends. The Fairythorn Tree chopped down? That would be a disaster!

Chapter 5

"It's been the worst Midsummer's morning ever," Fleur groaned.

"Except for that one when there was no rain for two full moons, and all the Bigs' flowers died," said Honeysuckle. "That was pretty nasty."

"At least everything grew back," said Fleur miserably. "Fairythorn Trees don't grow on… well… trees! It takes ages and ages and a ton of powerful magic to grow a new one."

She glanced over at Red, playing happily with the other draglings, unaware of the threat to their home. The sun had grown hotter still, though it wasn't even lunchtime yet. The sheaves of wheat in the fields behind the garden were buckling over as if they were trying to hide from the sun's hot rays.

"If that rotten Big cuts our home down, where are we supposed to live?" said Posy. "There are hundreds of us!"

"Mother Nature wouldn't leave us homeless," said Rose. "She'd find somewhere for us to live and work."

"It wouldn't be the same, though, would it?" whispered Fleur as she gazed at their tree fondly. "It wouldn't be home."

The tree looked ordinary from the outside, as did every Fairythorn. But inside, magically hidden within the trunk and branches, was an amazing network of tunnels and rooms. Every fairy had their own bedroom, but there were also shared rooms for hanging out, and classrooms where fairies could learn about things like caring for draglings and colour blending for wild flowers.

The Fairythorn Tree was a safe and secret place for the fairies who lived in the Bigs' world. Fleur loved it, especially at night, when it sparkled with rainbows of light.

The fairies had decorated all the walls and every free corner with shiny bits and other pretty things they had gathered from the Bigs' garden.

In dark corners, small balls of fairy fire floated in the air, making everything glow. Fleur couldn't bear the thought that with a few swings of a Big's axe, it would all be gone.

"I've just had a horrible thought..." Rose yelped. "What if Mother Nature splits us up?"

"What do you mean?" asked Posy.

"Well, there are loads of other Fairythorn Trees in the Bigs' world," said Rose. "But I bet they've got lots of fairies living in them already. There might not be enough room to move all of us together."

"Maybe Mother Nature will send us all back to live in Fairyland," Posy suggested. "I guess that would be okay, but I do like it here." She fluttered her purple wings. "Especially now I've got these to fly about w—"

She stopped herself. "Oh! I'm sorry, Fleur and Honeysuckle... I've put my fairy foot in it, haven't I?"

"Don't be silly," said Fleur. Not having her wings yet didn't seem quite as important as before. "And I know what you mean," she continued. "In Fairyland, everything is magical, but here in the Bigs' world, the magic is sort of spread out. When you find a little bit of something magical, it makes it more special, somehow."

"And I really love my room," Posy said. Then her eyes widened and she clapped a hand over her mouth. "Oh, Honeysuckle, I'm so sorry. I forgot! Again. I'm so stupid…"

Honeysuckle shrugged. "It's okay," she said. "Losing my room is nothing compared to losing the whole tree."

At that moment, the back door of the Bigs' house flew open again, and the fairies quickly ducked out of sight behind a tree root. It was Alice this time, thank goodness. She was wearing a pair of jeans and a bright-pink T-shirt with a picture of a bicycle on the front.

"Oh good," Fleur said. "A nice Big." She poked her head out over the top of the twisted root and frowned. "But what's she up to?"

Alice had a red sleeping bag and a stripy cushion in

her arms. She marched down to the bottom of the garden and dropped them on the grass. Then she sprinted over to the shed and slipped inside, banging the door shut behind her.

"What *is* she doing?" asked Posy.

The shed door swung open and Alice came out, her dad following. Fleur's heart skipped a beat – was he going to chop the tree down right away? Mr Miller was carrying a tent and was muttering loudly about lost pegs.

Meanwhile, Alice had a little peg bag in one hand and a yellow plastic mallet in the other. They walked over to the spot where Alice had dropped her sleeping bag and cushion, then Alice's dad began to unroll the tent.

"If your mother put things away properly, we wouldn't keep losing everything," Mr Miller grumbled. "She left the car keys in the freezer last week."

"I think we've got enough pegs here anyway, Dad," said Alice as she shook out the bag onto the grass. "See, there's loads."

"Looks like Alice is camping in the garden tonight," whispered Rose.

The fairies watched as the Bigs put up the tent. Alice handed Mr Miller the pegs and he hammered them into the ground.

"Hey, what's that?" Alice was pointing at the lumpy potato sack under the tree. She left her dad to finish off the tent and skipped over to the Fairythorn. When she lifted the sack to see two miserable-looking concrete gnomes, she burst out laughing.

"I bet Mum did this to you, didn't she, Mr Gnome?" Alice grinned. "She's not exactly your biggest fan."

"Join the club," muttered Fleur under her breath.

Then Alice's smile faded. "What happened here?" she called to her dad as she walked over to the broken Fairythorn Tree branch. She knelt down beside it, and ran a hand over the splintered, jagged end of the broken branch.

Mr Miller glanced up. His face was red and sweaty and his glasses had slipped to the end of his nose.

"I'm clearing a space for my new shed," he called back, shoving his glasses back into place.

Alice gasped. "Not here, Dad! No way! I love this tree. You can't!"

"Go, little Big!" whispered Fleur, punching the air. "At least someone's fighting for us."

"Sorry, Alice," Mr Miller said, standing up. "It's the best spot for it. My mind's made up."

"But, Dad… me and Edie think it's a fairy tree," said Alice. "If fairies live in it, you can't cut it down or you'll get really bad luck – for ever!"

Mr Miller rolled his eyes. "And I suppose Jack Frost is living under my rose bush, is he?" he teased.

"For Grot's sake, how stupid is that Big," Posy snorted. "Everyone knows Jack spends his summers at the North Pole."

"Dad," Alice continued, "fairies are real. I've seen them." She hurried back to Mr Miller and the tent. "They helped me find Edie and they left us the wildflower seeds that made the garden so pretty."

Mr Miller looked at the garden. "And a very nice job they did too," he muttered. "But, seriously," he said, turning to Alice, "unless your fairies start paying rent, they had better start looking for a new home as of tomorrow morning. Because that's when I'm chopping the tree down, like it or not."

Chapter 6

Alice and her dad walked back to the house, arguing about the tree as they went. Fleur turned to her friends, feeling cold with fear.

"But tomorrow is only one moon away!" she said. "What are we going to do?"

"Start packing?" Clive suggested.

"Shut it," said Fleur, "or the sack goes back."

Honeysuckle let out a little sigh.

"I don't even have anything to pack any more," she said miserably. "This is all so horrible."

"I don't want to move," said Rose, and a big fat

teardrop ran down her cheek. "I'm already feeling homesick, and we haven't gone anywhere yet."

There were other fairies who had overheard Mr Miller, too. They were gathering around the foot of the Fairythorn Tree, talking in low, worried voices. Even the draglings

had stopped larking about and had settled quietly beside their fairies.

Fleur rubbed Red's nose as he nuzzled against her. She could sense something else was wrong, but in the chaos of fairies worrying about the tree, she couldn't quite work out what.

Just then, a huge hydrangea bush near the pond started to shake and rustle.

"Watch out," said Posy, ducking out of sight again. "There's a Big in the bush."

Alice's best friend, Edie, stepped out from a gap in the shrubs, picking leaves from her wild black hair. She had a little green rucksack strapped to her back, and was struggling to hold on to a sleeping bag as well as a huge blue torch.

Alice came dashing out of the house and down the path to join her friend. She was carrying a basket which jangled and clinked as she hurried along.

"Mum gave me these jam jars for later," she explained, setting the basket down next to the tent. "They've got tea-light candles in them. But they're for outside only. Dad said we have to call Mum when we want to light them and we mustn't put them in the tent."

"Okay!" said Edie, slipping off the rucksack. She held up the torch. "I got this out of my brothers' room. I'd have asked permission, but they'd only have said no. They'll kill me if they find out." She grinned cheerfully. "And look what else I've got."

The girls sat down on the grass, and Edie poured the contents of her bag onto the ground. As well as her pyjamas, there were pens and notepads, two packets of chocolate buttons, a large stone with a hole through its middle, a pair of plastic binoculars and a disposable camera.

The chocolate didn't last long.

"What's this stone for?" mumbled Alice through a chocolatey mouthful. She held it up to her eye and peered through the hole.

"You can see fairies through them if you're in the right spot and they happen to be there. Which they will be because it's Midsummer's Day and everyone knows that's the best time to see fairies ever," Edie explained, emptying crumbs of chocolate from the packet into her cupped hand. "Mum helped me look up loads of stuff on the Internet so we'd be extra ready. If we want to see our fairies again, tonight's the night."

"No, it's not," moaned Posy. "And you won't see us ever again if we have to move out of the Fairythorn!"

Edie grabbed a notepad and opened it up.

"The best time to see fairies is at dusk," she read from her notes, "but if we rub fern seeds on our eyelids then we get fairy sight, which means we'll be able to see them all night long."

She peered at Alice over the top of her notepad. "If we can't find fern seeds we can brew up a mixture of rosemary, thyme and primroses with spring water. But pond water will do."

"I think we should use tap water," said Alice, peering over at the murky pond. "We can get the herbs from the kitchen and there are primroses all over the garden, so that part is easy. What else?"

"Well – this is important – we mustn't eat any of their food, or we'll be stuck with them for seven years."

"I don't mind that," said Alice. "I wouldn't mind having fairies hanging around for ever."

"They don't hang around, silly," said Edie. "They take you to Fairyland. You have to stay there."

"That sounds mean. Why would they keep someone prisoner like that?"

"I dunno," said Edie. "Maybe

fairy food is poisonous to humans and they have to take you to Fairyland to make you better."

Alice popped her last chocolate button into her mouth and licked her fingertips.

Edie looked back down at her notepad. "And we have to make a ring of stones around the tent and sit with our eyes half open, staring at a spot under a big tree – the fairy tree."

"I almost forgot!" Alice said, spluttering chocolate everywhere. "Edie, Dad wants to cut down our tree. He wants to build a new shed there!"

Edie looked at the existing shed. "But he's already got one," she said. "And where will the fairies live?"

"Exactly!" said Alice. "That's what I've been saying, but I don't think he's taking me seriously." She shrugged. "I'm trying to make him change his mind, but he doesn't believe in fairies and says that his shed is more important than an ugly old tree."

From behind the tree roots, the fairies shook with annoyance.

"Ugly old tree?" gasped Fleur, clenching her fists.

Meanwhile, Edie pulled a face

and tutted. "It's not ugly. Grown-ups are so silly sometimes," she said.

"Tell me about it!" agreed Alice, rolling her eyes.

They stared over at the tree, sadly, and were quiet for a few moments.

"We have to stop him!" said Edie suddenly. "There must be a way."

Just then, the kitchen window opened and Mrs Miller stuck her head out. "What would you like for lunch, girls?" she shouted. "Cheese on toast?"

"Yes, please, Mum," Alice shouted back, as Edie nodded enthusiastically.

"Come inside then, girls," Mrs

Miller called. "It'll be ready in five."

The fairies stepped out from their hiding place as soon as Alice and Edie had disappeared into the house. Red, Pax, Dash and Pip came barrelling out of a straggly strawberry patch nearby.

Fleur could tell they'd been stuffing themselves with the plump red berries – their fur was sticky from the juice and they were covered in pips.

"It's a shame we might not be around for the little Bigs' fairy hunt later," said Rose sadly. "It sounds like fun."

"Who knows where we'll be," sighed Honeysuckle.

"Right here if the little Bigs have got anything to do with it," said Fleur. "Just you wait and see. I know they won't let us down."

Fleur stopped and listened. Then

she covered her ears and opened and closed her mouth, and shook her head from side to side. "Can anyone else hear a buzzing noise?" she asked.

The four fairies looked around, and then Posy pointed at the tree. "Oh no…" she said. "Look!"

Fleur glanced up to see a little swarm of angry bees. They were flying in and out of their nest and seemed in a state of terrible excitement.

"What's got them so cross?" asked Fleur. "They were fine this morning."

"Argh! Of course!" Rose cried,

slapping her forehead. "Their nest is just above the branch that the Big destroyed. I bet it's got them in a real tizz."

Fleur nodded, her eyes wide. "Yes, they hate being disturbed. We should have noticed earlier!"

"I'll go and see if I can calm them down," Posy said, and flew up to the nest.

Posy held out her hands to soothe the angry worker bees who met her. But although she could usually calm the most bad-tempered of creatures, it didn't look like Posy was going to have any luck with the bees.

After a few minutes, Posy fluttered back to the others on her purple wings, and shook her head.

"It's no good!" she said. "They are really cross. I can't calm them down, no matter what I say. I'm worried they're going to create a giant swarm and start attacking anything that comes near."

"You're right, Posy," Rose said. "It's not like them – they're usually so gentle – but if they get really angry, there's no telling what they'll do."

The fairies looked at each other,

frowning. They had to help the bees, but how? "Mother Nature's going to be really unhappy," said Rose. "Even if they don't swarm, how will we harvest honey for our feast if the bees are all cross and grizzly?"

"We won't be able to," said Posy. "They're not going to let anyone in right now."

"We've got to do something," said Honeysuckle. "They seem to be getting angrier by the second!" The bees were now circling the tree, round and round, going so fast that they were just a stripy blur.

Fleur sucked in a breath. She knew something that might calm the bees. They always loved the dawn chorus. But would she really dare?

"I could..." Fleur began.

"... sing?" finished Posy. "Yes, oh, yes please!"

"You have to try, Fleur," said Rose, her deep brown eyes pleading.

Fleur dropped her head. "But what if something terrible happens?"

"Something terrible is already happening!" Honeysuckle exclaimed.

"Please sing to the bees, Fleur," said Rose. "It'll be the Midsummer

Feast soon and it could be our last one here together, but it won't go ahead with the bees in this state."

Fleur looked round at her friends' anxious faces. She knew they were counting on her, but she hadn't tried to sing for so long that she didn't even know if she could.

"What if I can't sing any more?" she said, holding her throat as if her voice might suddenly burst out and run away.

Posy shrugged. "You won't know if you don't try," she said. "Go on, Fleur, give it a shot. We could gather the Choir Fairies, but you've got the best voice out of everyone, and you can do it right now. What do you say?"

"Please?" begged Honeysuckle. "It's been such a horrible day."

That was it. Fleur couldn't refuse Honeysuckle, not after she had lost all of her precious belongings. "Okay," she nodded. "I'll give it a go."

Fleur cleared her throat and concentrated. She felt the music well up inside her, like she was a balloon being filled, and she opened her mouth.

But nothing came out.

Chapter 7

"Oh no!" squeaked Fleur. "You were right, Honeysuckle. I've let my singing voice get small and skinny and now there's nothing left!"

Rose shook her head. "You've just forgotten how to use it," she said. "Give it another go."

Fleur nodded and took a deep breath. She knew Rose was right – her singing voice was still inside. It was a part of her, like her elbow or her nose.

Nothing could change that.

She opened her mouth wide and closed her eyes, but again, nothing came out. Fleur stared at her friends in silent shock. Red bounded over and threaded himself between her ankles.

"Maybe it's nerves," suggested Honeysuckle.

"Or maybe it's stuck in your throat," said Posy. "Would it help if we turned you upside down and shook it out?"

Fleur shrugged miserably. "Worth a try, I suppose." She dusted her palms together and prepared to perform a handstand.

But then a sudden breeze swept over the garden, ruffling all the leaves and petals, and making Fleur stop in her tracks. For a split second, the sun seemed to flare even brighter and a golden ball of light appeared in front of the Fairythorn Tree, making all the fairies in the garden sparkle.

From out of the ball of golden light came a cloud of butterflies. Then they parted like a curtain and all the fairies gasped as Mother Nature stepped out into the world.

She was incredibly beautiful, with hair the colour of autumn leaves that tumbled around her shoulders like a waterfall. She was wearing a spectacular Midsummer crown made from eagle feathers and tiger lilies. Her eyes were the same deep green as a warm summer sea and her skin was as pale as sunlight on snow.

The fairies and creatures of the

garden hurried over, just to be near her.

"I'm afraid a handstand won't work," said Mother Nature gently. "Fleur, music comes from the heart. Try thinking about something that is special to you. Use your voice to express your feelings."

Mother Nature reached up and plucked a sunbeam straight out of the air, as if it were a long sheet of silk. She shook it and Fleur watched in awe as the golden beam stretched and shaped itself into a shimmering staircase. The glistening stairs led from the foot of the Fairythorn Tree right up to the bees' nest. Mother Nature nodded at Fleur and smiled encouragingly again.

"Go on," she said. "Why don't you climb those stairs and tell the bees how you feel."

Fleur stared at the sunbeam staircase and went weak at the knees.

"It's just like breathing, remember?" Rose said, gently nudging her friend towards the foot of the stairs. "You were born to sing, Fleur."

"Good luck!" Posy called. "And don't forget to ask about the honey, we still need it for the Midsummer Feast!"

"Maybe now's not the time for that, Posy," said Fleur with a nervous grin, then she spun on her heels and raced up the sunbeam staircase with

Red scampering close behind.

The bees' furious buzzing got louder the higher she climbed. It roared like motorway traffic, but Fleur fought the urge to cover her ears. She reached the top of the staircase and steadied herself with one hand against the trunk.

She peered down at the ground, far below. Her friends were waving up at her madly, and other fairies and their draglings had gathered to watch, too. Everyone was expecting her to sing.

"No pressure, then," Fleur muttered. "Oh, Red! They're all

counting on me, but I don't think I can do it." Red nuzzled into his mistress's leg and purred. "I can't even think of a song to sing," said Fleur.

Then something surprising happened.

Draglings aren't exactly known for their sweet singing voices. But that didn't stop Red. He sat back on his hindlegs, threw back his head and sang. It was awful! Like a cross between a frog and chainsaw.

The buzzing stopped for a moment, as if the bees had been stunned into silence, then it started up again, even louder than before. But that didn't stop Red – in fact, he puffed out his chest and sang even louder.

"What are you doing, boy?" laughed Fleur. She eyed the bees nervously. "I'm not sure you're helping." But Red kept up his dreadful screeching. Fleur turned to him and suddenly realised what he was doing. Through the noise she had recognised a snippet of a tune.

"Our song!" she cried out in delight. "You remembered it, Red."

Red carried on wailing cheerfully while Fleur listened, smiling. She'd forgotten all about the song she used to sing to Red every morning when they woke up. She thought back to those happy sunlit mornings in the Fairythorn Tree.

"That's not quite it," she said absent-mindedly, still lost in her daydream. "It goes like this."

And without even thinking about it, Fleur began to sing:

We all live in the Fairythorn Tree,
Warm and safe and happy as can be.
We work and play and sing all day,
And chase the Grot Goblins away!

Fleur hadn't noticed that Red had stopped his own awful singing to listen to hers.

She didn't see the audience below the tree, craning to hear her and swaying together on the lawn. And she didn't spot the flying fairies or the birds who settled in the branches around her, just to hear her better. She didn't even notice when the bees finally fell silent. Fleur was simply lost in happy thoughts about the Fairythorn Tree, and the words of the song rushed straight from her heart and out into the world.

We'll never stray from our Fairythorn home,

For while you're here you're never alone.

Surrounded by your family

In the wonderful, magical Fairythorn Tree.

The last line caught in Fleur's throat as she remembered the Big's terrible plan. She snapped out of her daydream and saw Red at her feet, looking very pleased with himself. The branches around them were crowded with creatures, all waiting, spellbound, for the next note.

"Bravo!" shouted Derek from the foot of the tree.

"It's *brava* for a girl," said Clive. "Delightful voice, though. I quite agree… Err… rubbish song though," he added with a sneer.

"Oh yes, obviously," sniffed Derek, his voice a bit wobbly. "What a load of twaddle."

The fairies burst into loud cheering. Fleur's mouth dropped

open in shock.
She'd done
it. She had
sung again.
And she'd
calmed the bees
down, too. Even the Queen Bee had
popped out to listen, which was a very
rare honour indeed. There would be
plenty of honey at the feast that night,
that was certain.

Fleur was just about to climb
back down the sunbeam staircase
when it happened. Suddenly, she felt
way too hot, even for a summer's day,

and her back was all itchy. She felt dizzy too, as if she'd just climbed off a roundabout.

She realised everyone was staring at her, but she didn't know what to do.

"What's going on...?" she asked, just as the tingling in her shoulders turned into a warm rush, and a familiar sound, like the ringing of a thousand tiny bells, filled the Midsummer air.

Chapter 8

With an almighty cloud of fairy dust, Fleur's wings exploded outwards in all directions, taking everyone by surprise. The wings were obviously as impatient as their owner. And what beautiful wings they were. Snow white, like high clouds on a summer day, except for the tips which flickered and sparkled with fiery colours.

"Wow!" said Fleur, bursting into laughter. "I wasn't expecting that!"

There was a short, sharp, dragling yelp and Red's fur puffed out like he'd had an electric shock. As it settled again, he changed colour, into a warm amber, with fiery red tips to his ears. He looked down at himself and purred with delight.

"You look amazing, Red," said Fleur, twisting round to try and get a better look at her new wings. "So do I... I think," she added, giggling with excitement.

"You can fly down by yourself now," Mother Nature called up from the ground.

Fleur grinned, held her wings outstretched and jumped from the sunshine staircase. She flapped her wings and shot upwards, like a rocket. It felt incredible, like jumping on a trampoline and never coming down.

Fleur laughed out loud as she soared above the branches of the tree and floated on the warm afternoon breeze. She smiled at Red, flying close by, and thought again about her song. It had felt good to let her voice fly free on the wind again, just as she was flying now. It felt right.

"I will never let anything stop

me from singing, ever again" she told herself firmly. Then she flipped over and darted down to her friends, clumsily crash-landing on the soft, shaggy lawn. Red landed rather more neatly behind her, and the other draglings flocked round to admire his new markings.

"You'll get used to the landing thing," said Posy, as she helped

Fleur to her feet. "It only gets easier, I promise. Your wings look wonderful."

"What, these old things?" Fleur joked.

"Congratulations, Fleur, you're a Song Fairy," announced a smiling Mother Nature. "Although, there was never really any doubt about that, was there?" she chuckled. "And now that you've realised how important your gift is, I look forward to hearing you sing with the choir. I've missed your lovely voice these past months."

"Thank you," said Fleur, blushing with pride.

"I'd better leave you to your Midsummer preparations," said Mother Nature. "I know you're worrying about the Fairythorn Tree, but we've got to celebrate first, and that can't be forgotten about. Goodbye for now, fairies, draglings and all my other friends – including you gnomes." She nodded to Derek and Clive, and if concrete could blush, they would have turned as red as radishes. "Happy Midsummer's Day to you all."

She walked over to the Fairythorn Tree and whispered something into a hollow in its trunk. Then she placed a hand on its rough, old bark. When she took her hand away, there was a perfect print left behind, in a darker shade to the bark around it.

"The sun sets only to rise again," Mother Nature said. "Remember that, fairies."

She clapped her hands. "Now each of you to your tasks, there's plenty to do before the feast!"

As she watched Mother Nature

leave, Fleur saw Honeysuckle's sad face in the corner of her eye. Fleur knew she was thinking about the broken branch, and her beloved bedroom. They all might soon be losing their home, but Fleur suddenly thought of something she could do to cheer her friend up.

And then, like fairy magic, something else caught her eye, something pink and shimmery, poking out from behind a patch of clover.

Fleur looked around quickly. Rose had linked arms with Honeysuckle, and they were heading off to help gather honey. So Fleur grabbed her chance and rushed over to Posy to whisper her plan in her friend's ear.

Chapter 9

Fleur and Posy had been busy on their secret mission and now there wasn't much time left before sunset. They both got busy in the Fairythorn kitchen, brewing great pots of refreshing mint tea and making bowls of dandelion salad and acorn pies.

As she worked, Fleur tried not to think about what would happen after the feast – having to find a new home. It was just too sad and too awful. Fleur hoped more than anything else that she and Rose and Honeysuckle and Posy would get to stay together, but she knew that it was not certain.

She gave herself a little shake as she almost dropped a pie, distracted by her thoughts. As Mother Nature had pointed out, there was a celebration that needed to happen. She'd worry about the Fairythorn Tree later.

Fleur looked around the kitchen. There was geranium-leaf sorbet with strawberry shortcake for pudding, and buckets and buckets of honey.

The bees had been very generous, and it had taken many fairies to help with the honey harvest. Honeysuckle and Rose brought in great baskets of it, grinning as they went. Fleur saw that their mouths were slightly shiny, and guessed they'd been eating it as they worked. She would have done the same thing – the honey was delicious!

Outside the Fairythorn Tree, the sun was a big splash of red in the sky as it sank closer and closer to the treetops.

It was a beautiful evening. A perfect ring of toadstools had sprung up around the fairies' feasting tables, which were laid out in rows on the grass beneath the Fairythorn. To anyone passing, the goings on inside the ring would be quite invisible.

Fleur grinned as she fluttered over to join her friends. Posy had already gone outside with Rose and Honeysuckle, as Fleur had had to go and pick up something from the bees after they left the Fairythorn kitchen.

Fleur didn't really need to fly such a short distance, but she just wanted to. With all the preparations, she hadn't had another chance for a proper fly yet. She longed to be up among the clouds again.

To mark the occasion, all the fairies wore their Midsummer crowns, which they'd been working on all spring — the bigger and fancier, the better.

Posy's crown was so big that she could barely move beneath it. She'd built it from radish leaves, bright yellow St John's Wort flowers and shiny black crow's feathers, and it was almost as tall as she was.

Honeysuckle's crown was much shorter, made quickly from brightly coloured sweet-pea petals after her oak-leaf crown had been crushed.

Rose had used fluffy yellow duckling feathers threaded with plastic pearls from a broken necklace.

Fleur had made her crown from white strawberry flowers and rich red clover, which now matched her new wings.

They'd all groomed their draglings, too – Fleur had brushed Red's new fur to a soft, shiny finish.

"That's quite a crown, Posy," said Fleur as she flopped down beside her.

"I could say the same about your wings," Posy grinned back. "And what about all this?" She pointed at everything in front of them. "Nice isn't it?"

"It's beautiful," sighed Fleur.

The fairies had scattered huge spider-silk rugs on the ground to create a dancefloor. Other fairies hovered overhead, stringing daisy-chain lanterns between the branches of the tree. Fortunately, Derek and Clive were having forty winks –

although their rattling snores were a bit annoying.

Further up the garden, the fairies could see that Alice and Edie were celebrating Midsummer too.

They'd laid stones in a circle around their tent. Edie was chattering about how the stones were sea urchin fossils that her family had collected on holiday. The tealights were lit and glowing in the jam jars. Multi-coloured bunting was tied around the tent ropes and the girls were wearing Midsummer crowns of their own, made from flowers picked in the Millers' back garden.

Fleur could see a tray, and on it was the stone with a hole in it, some water in a bowl, a camera, and some binoculars. There was also lots of food – crisps and biscuits and bananas.

"It's so we're not tempted if a fairy offers us something to eat," Alice told Edie.

"What are the little Bigs up to now?" Posy asked Fleur, fluttering over to her side.

Alice and Edie had scrambled to their feet and were coming towards the Fairythorn Tree. Alice's crown of flowers kept slipping down over her eyes and Edie was giggling and tapping her friend on the head with a plastic wand.

Fortunately, the toadstool fairy ring did its job, and the girls didn't notice the hundreds of tiny fairies who were getting ready for the party of the year, right under their very noses.

Alice and Edie knew that a few fairies lived in the garden – earlier that summer, Rose had revealed herself to Alice to help her make friends with

Edie. But the girls would have had quite a shock if they had known just how many fairies there really were!

"Where shall we put them then?" asked Alice. She wriggled her bare toes, pointing them in the direction of the toadstool circle. "It looks like the fairies have been here already."

"Don't panic," Fleur told Posy, who jumped up when Alice pointed her toes at the toadstools. "They can't see inside the circle, remember?"

"It doesn't matter *where* we put them," said Edie. "It just said we have to tie a rag or a ribbon to the branches of a Fairythorn Tree and then we can make a wish."

Alice and Edie reached into their pockets and each pulled out a strip of an old bedsheet.

Fleur nudged Rose, the Wish Fairy. "Over to you, Rose."

Rose sprang to her feet, ready for duty. As long as a Big made a wish with goodness in their heart, she would be able to grant it.

"Okay," said Alice.

She tied her strip of sheet to a low branch and squeezed her eyes shut tight. "I wish that my dad would decide not to cut down the fairy tree."

Fleur gasped. "Did she really just wish that?"

Edie tied her piece of sheet to a branch next to Alice's. "And I wish he wouldn't cut it down too."

Fleur watched in excitement as Rose began sparkling from head to toe. Then just as suddenly as it started, the sparkling stopped.

"Is that it?" said Posy.

Rose shrugged. "What do you want, fireworks?"

"But has it worked?" asked Honeysuckle.

They all waited for something to happen. Nothing did.

Then Rose gave a little smile, and a big wink. "You'll just have to wait a bit longer, then we'll see," she said.

Chapter 10

The fairies weren't the only ones waiting for something magical to happen. Alice and Edie stood under the tree, staring hopefully at their wish rags.

"Do you think it will work?" asked Alice, tugging at the bottom of her scrap of bedsheet. "I'm not really sure how tying rags to it is going to change Dad's mind."

"You've got to believe in magic

for it to work," said Edie. "And we believe in it, don't we?"

"Of course," Alice nodded. "But Dad doesn't, and he's the one it needs to work on."

The two girls crouched down in the grass. "Here," said Edie, taking the holey stone from her pocket and passing it to Alice. "It's meant to give you fairy sight. Can you see them through it?"

Alice held it up to her eye, staring through it, right at the tuft of grass where Fleur and her friends were standing. "No," she said. "All I can see are the toadstools, and the grass!" She hung her head.

"Why can't we see the fairies today?" Edie wondered out loud. "Let me have a go."

But she was soon shaking her head and pocketing the stone. "You're right – there's nothing!"

"Our wish will never work if they're not even there," said Alice, sighing.

"Well, that's weird," said Fleur, turning to her friends. "How come the little Bigs can't see us, tonight of all nights?"

"Has it got something to do with your wish spell, Rose?" said Honeysuckle.

But Rose said nothing. The fairies knew she couldn't reveal a wish until it was granted.

"It could be some sort of special magic," suggested Posy. "Things do get a bit mixed up at Midsummer."

"Hang on," said Edie.

She raced over to the tent and grabbed the bowl of cloudy water. She scampered back, slopping most of the murky brew over the lawn as she hurried along.

"Here, Alice, put some of this on," she said, handing the bowl to her friend. "But make sure you don't get any of it in your eyes."

Both girls dipped their fingers into the bowl and rubbed the potion carefully on their eye lids. They crouched down again and stared hard at the ring of toadstools.

"Remember to look at one spot with your eyes half closed," said Edie.

They picked a spot and squinted into the gloom.

"Can't see anything," said Alice, forlornly. "Can you?"

"Nope," sighed Edie. "But that doesn't mean they're not there," she added, hopefully.

Alice looked like she was about to burst into tears. Fleur wished there was something she could do.

But at that moment, the Bigs' back door flew open and out charged Mr Miller, a pair of binoculars in one hand and a book in another.

"Cuckoo! Cuckoo!" cried Mr Miller, flapping his arms and running down the garden. "Cuckoo!"

"What the dandelion clock is going on?" said Fleur, turning to Rose.

"Er, Dad, are you okay?" Alice asked.

"Cuckoo!" he cried again, then pointed at the top of the Fairythorn Tree. "Up there! A Great Spotted Cuckoo! Look!"

Alice and Edie followed Mr Miller's gaze to the top of the tree.

Fleur looked up too. There, at the very top of the Fairythorn Tree, a new bird had taken up residence. A Great Spotted Cuckoo! She'd never met any before, but she knew they were incredibly rare.

"Rose," she said. "Is that part of the wish?"

"Shhh," whispered Honeysuckle, watching what the Bigs did next.

Mr Miller stared up at the tree, his neck craned. "It's my favourite bird," he explained to Alice and Edie, who were jumping up and down, trying to get a look at the bird in the high branches. "But I've never seen one before – let alone in my own garden!"

Fleur saw Alice's eyes light up with hope.

"I think it's living in the tree, Dad," she said.

"Yes, Mr Miller," agreed Edie. "It looks really happy up there."

The Great Spotted Cuckoo was fluttering about in the uppermost branches. Fleur saw that it had a yellow face and whiteish tummy, with a grey back and wings that were spotted with white.

She took a deep breath, waiting

for what the biggest Big would say next.

"This changes everything," Mr Miller said at last. "The tree is going nowhere!" He held his binoculars up to his eyes, shaking his head and smiling as he looked at the bird close up.

"Hurrah!" Alice and Edie shouted together.

"I don't really need a new shed, anyway," Mr Miller continued. "The old one will do nicely. I might think about converting the loft instead."

He moved back towards the open kitchen door without lowering his binoculars. "A Great Spotted Cuckoo! I must tell your mum about this…"

As the biggest Big disappeared inside, cheers rang out in the garden from fairies and little Bigs alike.

"Our wish worked!" cried Alice, as the two girls skipped around their tent. "The fairies must be there, after all!"

Fleur turned to her fairy friends and grinned. The little Bigs were happy – and so were the fairies. The Fairythorn Tree was saved!

Chapter 11

While the little Bigs enjoyed their camping sleepover, the fairies had their Midsummer Feast. And as the sun finally set, Fleur joined the choir on a tree branch, her stomach

fluttering with nerves. But as soon as she started singing the sunset song with her fellow Song Fairies, her nerves disappeared, and she thought her heart might burst with happiness.

The feast was a huge success, and with the threat to their tree now gone, the fairies danced and sang and laughed late into the night.

As the four fairy friends danced and twirled together, Fleur felt so happy – it really was the perfect ending to Midsummer's Day. And she couldn't wait to sing with the choir again in the morning!

Fleur got up early the next day. Dawn was about to appear, and the sky was a mixture of pale starlight and a warm orange and red glow. But before she joined the rest of the Sunrise Choir, who were already gathering along the branches of the Fairythorn Tree, she had something very important to do.

Fleur found Honeysuckle in Rose's bedroom, rubbing the sleep out of her eyes. She handed her friend a small parcel. It was squishy and light, wrapped in a shiny green oak leaf and tied up with spider silk.

"Ooh…what's this?" Honeysuckle asked.

"Just a little something to make you smile," said Fleur, grinning. "Open it." She could hear the Choir Fairies outside, clearing their throats and warming up their voices with scales. "But you'd better hurry up, I've got a job to go to."

Honeysuckle ripped open the oak-leaf parcel and let out a squeal of delight so shrill that it woke up Derek and Clive, out in the garden. They started moaning immediately.

"Now what?" muttered Derek.

"It's all go around this flamin' tree. I miss the pond."

"The sooner someone moves us back, the better," grumbled Clive. "What time do you call this? It's not even dawn! I need my beauty sleep."

"Bit late for that," laughed Honeysuckle, as she hugged her new ballet shoes to her chest. They looked

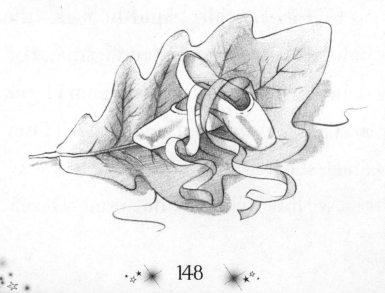

just like her old favourites!

"How did you do it, Fleur?" Honeysuckle asked. "They're perfect!"

"I found a piece of a silk scarf in the garden," Fleur told her, "Posy helped me design it into a new pair of shoes, and the bees used their honey to glue the silk together."

Honeysuckle threw her arms around Fleur's neck and hugged her tightly. "Thank you, Fleur," she said.

The twinkle was back in Honeysuckle's eyes for the first time since she'd lost her bedroom. "Now you've got a job to do, remember?"

Honeysuckle shooed her friend away. "Go and sing for us!"

Fleur didn't need telling twice. She dashed out of the Fairythorn Tree and leapt into the air, leaving a trail of glittering fairy dust behind her.

She flew up and up and up, then landed on the choir's branch and took her place in the line of Song Fairies with great pride.

Red settled on a nearby twig, and Fleur gave her dragling a quick smile. Her precious companion was never far away.

Fleur spotted her friends, who'd come out to watch her first sunrise performance, and they waved back eagerly. Her heart filled with love and happiness. The sun peaked over the horizon just as she opened her mouth to sing.

And afterwards, everyone agreed that the sunrise song that morning was the loveliest sound they had ever heard.

Rose

Rose is kind, sensitive
and gentle. She's
always trying to
make things better
for those around her,
but is also a worrier.
She likes sparkly things,
flower petals and weaving
decorations into her hair.

Posy

Posy is unstoppable
and brave. She
adores animals and
is often found riding
butterflies or chatting
to squirrels. Posy loves
to wear feathers and
her clothes are mainly
assembled from things
she finds in nature.

Honeysuckle

Honeysuckle is a dreamer. She's a bit dizzy and clumsy, but very sweet with it. She has boundless energy and loves to dance among the flowers, releasing their scent as she pirouettes from bloom to bloom.

Fleur

Fleur is feisty, funny, fiery and cool. Her striking red hair twinkles with tiny stars and her eyes are always changing colour. She loves music and singing. Fleur can make a musical instrument from anything she finds, especially natural things.